W9-BAU-548

goodbye, hello

by Robert Welber

Illustrations by Cyndy Szekeres

Pantheon Books

For the children, parents, and staff
of
The Studio on Eleventh Street

 Published in the United States by Pantheon Books, a division of Random House, Inc., and simultaneously in Canada by Random House of Canada Limited, Toronto. Manufactured in the United States of America. (CIP on last page.)

A kitten goes creeping
away from the rug.
Goodbye Mother . . .

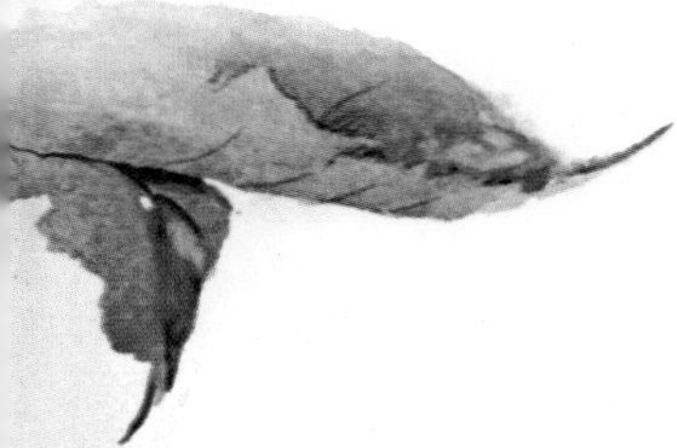

Hello bug.

A puppy goes sniffing
down the road.
Goodbye Mother...

Hello toad.

A mouse goes out
to climb and see.
Goodbye Mother...

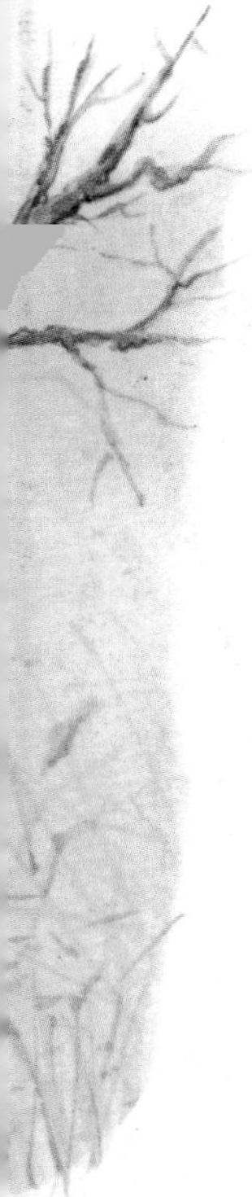

Hello tree.

A bird begins
to try to fly.
Goodbye Mother...

Hello sky.

A squirrel comes running
down the tree.
Goodbye Mother...

Hello bee.

A rabbit hops
out of a hole.
Goodbye Mother…

Hello mole.

A child is watching
each little creature.
Goodbye Mother…

Hello teacher.

Robert Welber, the author of *Frog, Frog, Frog, The Winter Picnic, The Train,* and *Song of the Seasons,* received his M.S. in Early Childhood and Elementary Education from the Bank Street College of Education. In 1971, after teaching both Nursery and Kindergarten in New York City, he founded his own school—The Studio on Eleventh Street, a one-room elementary school where children learn from each other and with guidance assume responsibility for their own education.

Cyndy Szekeres is well-known for her irresistible animal characters. She has illustrated over thirty picture books, including *Pippa Mouse* and *Moon Mouse,* an AIGA award-winner. She is also the creator of the popular *Cyndy's Animal Calendars* and *Cyndy's Workbook Diary.* She lives on a farm in Vermont with her husband, Gennaro Prozzo, a graphic artist, and their children Marc and Chris.

Library of Congress Cataloging in Publication Data
Welber, Robert. Goodbye, hello. SUMMARY: Pictures and rhymed text explore the idea that all young things must be independent sooner or later. [1. Stories in rhyme] I. Szekeres, Cyndy, illus. II. Title. PZ8.3.W429Go [E] 74-149
ISBN 0-394-82770-8 ISBN 0-394-92770-2 (lib. bdg.) 0 9 8 7 6 5 4 3 2 1